PRETTY OBSCURE

AN ANTHOLOGY

Published Exclusively and Globally by Far West Press

www.farwestpress.com

ISBN 979-8-9887354-4-1

Printed in the United States of America

Co-Editors: Willie Crane & Parker Love Bowling

Cover Art: Johnny Scuotto

THE MISTRESS OF MARVIN GARDENS

by Parker Love Bowling

I'm always naked, and
I am always pretty.
I am rarely honest, though
I am always sincere.
I do have a heart, no
matter how small
and my feelings get hurt
quite easily, and
often.

I am always naked, when
I awake,
showing the morning
my bare face

Bury my eyelashes of mink
in the sand
Burn my nighties, so
I may
remain naked, and

Sincere.

I SENT YOU A DREAM

by Craig Dyer

I sent you a dream
How was it received?
What it contained
Now only half comes to me

I believe in the beginning
Another took my hand
But I slipped out of a side door
In earnest search of you

You, the human thunderstorm
That through the dull, drab darkness of life
Rains down upon and illuminates
As your bolts of colourful lightning strike

What remains of the dream I sent you
Now appears torn at the edges
If only there were more time
for such whispered confidences

AMISSING
by David Erdos

And so London Field's fucked sky is sealed
As Martin/John Self is blue-pencilled, returning him
To Sally, his sister, his father and to Christopher
Hitchens,
His friend. And dead from the same disease too.
This is the sort of thing which would have befallen
Keith Talent, if he had been supported by the spell
Of his surname, and yet perhaps no name alone

Can defend against the onslaught of fate;
Indiscriminate, unexpected, with oesophageal cancer
Death's herald, as it was for Harold and for
Christopher H;
Writers throats proving to be the weak heel which
first
Tripped Achilles, before toppling the towers
From which these wizards with words met their moat;
The one we all sail when the Ferryman's oar

Taps our shoulder. Amis would have known.
He was knowing. Opinion infused all his prose.
From The Rachel Papers straight through to his last
Inside Story; an autobiographical excavation
Which he labelled a novel, as if in his dying the body
Characterised and reported incident and indictment,
While fear could not stifle the richness and way

His words flowed. Amis was eight parts mainstream
And two, or maybe three counter-culture. As
Kingsley's kid,
The young rebel sought to unseat state and quo

With constant critique. Martin as self-made sage
Was prolific, both in print and as pundit,
A TV interviewee who said no to the way
That things were, as he made prose seem psychedelic,

Or perhaps progressive, as he was both lumpen
And light frequently. And yet his books are also bright
Coral reefs through which the reader swims,
glimpsing
Wonders; whether it's the jargon and jive within
Money,
Time's Arrow's smooth horrors, or the spectacular
stories
Inside Einstein's Monsters which bellow
Like Bellow and teach writing itself what to be.
Amis used language like charge, amping up sense
And syntax. His sentences were set to eleven as he
rocked
And roared through his books. He was not as
dangerous
As he dared, for nepotistic or not, his position was
easier
To source and find than for we others who labour
alone
While the literati, Illuminati-like avoid hooks. And
yet
For artists my age, Amis was also a kind of glam-rock
institution,

More of a Bolan than a Bowie, while slyly epitomising
His time. Hitchens defiantly rioted and bore a taint
Of Hendrix about him, and yet Amis and McEwen,
(John Cale-like in his stories) pre-dated punk's
clamour

As each in turn would define literary success, along
With others like Ackroyd, Rushdie, James, Fenton,
Not rebels as such, but a team of societal satirists,

A batch of Peter Cooks in word kitchens, boiling up
Books and bathos, with notions and potions
Which could redden the route of mainstreams.
Martin Amis was also a grand soloist, if not on guitar
Then on keyboards. If I swap genres, he became
A kind of Rick Wakeman overdoing the phrase,
But replete with complete mastery of page as stage

For performance in which point, if not plot
Was proven under the glittering cape of technique.
His books were unique. He wanted to be the English
Updike, or Bellow. Nabokov, Burgess, or Ballard;
Each one of these men his work stalked. Well,
Time will tell. His books are escapade
And entertainment. Sermons from Martin's

Mount Olympus, via Notting Hill and New York.
Fat phrases spun from a slightly built man,
Whose voice sounded like a kind of whine
As he eyed you, his gimlet view brimming
As he questioned each day with high talk.
But now his death marks another peg freed
From the circus tent world I grew up in.

As Chat GPT can write novels and albums, too,
By which words will we set the state, whether quoed
Or not, we can follow to either measure attainment
Or equivocate with the birds as we soar above
Expectation and standard. As of now Martin's
missing.

So what is amiss? The absurd. And the state we're
All in, as idiots and AI overtakes us. As we search

For pleasure, we actually forgoe happiness. And all
For some distant dream that we do not know how
To capture. Perhaps when thinkers die they locate it.
Under spectacular skies, pages fountain, their streams
Feeding futures. Perhaps this is where Martin is.
For now, we will no longer hear of his teeth,
Or of his cousin Lucy, one of Fred West's first victims;

We will no longer remember a London which sparked
And fizzed, clinked and fused with Fitzgerald's New
York,
Or even Hemingway's Paris, not that Martin had
glamour,
But from such spill he sourced clues which led
To the great mystery of why it is people ruin every
chance
Granted and why in time we abuse not only the hand
That first helped and held us, but also the sentence

He devotedly served through each ruse.
He was a writer who won, and who in the fight
With style stayed triumphant. Like him or not,
Martin's talent – unlike his character, Keith's can
amuse.
As well as reveal the dark and dare in our standing.
In sitting down Amis travelled as far as words go.

So, salut.

21/5/23

CANDID NIGHT

by Dylan Lusetich

The night we spoke candidly
Removed of any ambiguity,
free of nuances and no paranoid compositions
nor inflections to take into account

Remember we drank all of your dad's wine
Gathered all our belongings and lit them on fire
took all my postcards of Golden Age actresses
jerked off over them and cried out

And hoped you'd hear it
and you said 'I've heard this all before'
and all the fog left my body
and my spirit rose to meet yours

And we danced and kissed
and we tripped on air
then looked down at my body
and I couldn't stop smiling

UNINTENTIONAL POEM HEARD ON TRI-MET WITH ACCELERATING SOCIAL COLLAPSE FRAME NEATLY IN EACH WINDOW LOOKING INSIDE AND OUT

by Kurt Eisenlohr

Force-feeding me those names
that are not mine and
never have been

Dottie!

Not my name
never me!

I don't answer to Dottie
the raspberry was damaged!

My name is Laurie
never Laura

That's recorded, Dottie!
Tangerines and elephants!

HUMOR WHISKEY

by Karen Schoemer

The phone plugs into the wall
When it rings no one answers it
I sleep on a cold stone monument
Black water drips over the edges

How would Charles Simic describe
the carpet with things spilled on it?
His spider lives in a corner
the one St. Veronica ate in her martyrdom

Great gods of hoops jump in green jerseys
Sticks in the ground dowser liquid astronauts
A drunk falls backwards over his shoelaces
Humor whiskey in the cupboard

I walk past your cluttered desk
It's still December
I can't move the calendar forward
I'm stuck in your orange paneled psychology

At a party
Where a hostess
Hands out canapes
In shot glasses

Dusty morsels
Of your death
My lips can't taste it
My heart isn't in it

Great gods of hoops jump in green jerseys

Sticks in the ground dowser liquid astronauts
A drunk falls backwards over his shoelaces
Hidden whiskey in the cupboard

You hated everything
I said it to you on the drive to Palm Springs
You hated me for saying it
The sun shone the sun shone on what?

You hated the sun
Hate blew in the windows like loose dirt from the hills
Your missing body dances and gets wasted
Shoot and miss shoot and miss shoot and hurt

Great gods of hoops jump in green jerseys
Sticks in the ground dowser liquid astronauts
A drunk falls backwards over his shoelaces
Humor whiskey hidden in the cupboard

Why did I say yes?
I don't want to be here
Surrounded by people I despise
Boat owners, Bertucci's brick oven pizza eaters

They feel sorry for me because you died
The phone rings, no one answers it
Someone tries the door from outside
but it's locked

ROACHES I HAVE KNOWN

by Jeffrey Wengrofsky

I can't tell you when I saw my first roach, but surely one saw me first. Roaches, spiders, ants, flies, and other wee-beasties that we only momentarily consider are usually still around, laying low, whether we notice them or not, silent and reluctant witnesses to our folly, deception, and bodily tinkering. Do they mock our gentilities, rolling sets of eyes or the insect equivalent, while we mop our kitchen floors or otherwise try to "clean" our nests? (What could "clean" mean to a roach? Malodorous? Poisonous? A food-desert? Humbuggery?)

Roaches took up residence in remotely primeval human dwellings, skittering along cave walls and poking antennae into our sleeping noses, long before cats and dogs became snuggly. Coevolving with us, they're clued-in enough to fear us. Unlike ants, bees, and termites enmeshed in the collective phantasmagoria of the hivemind, roaches will likely notice you noticing them. And if they are any more intelligent than they seem, it would probably be in their interest to hide it from us, so who's to know? Moreover, the ordinary roach has a skill set that would put all the Bond villains to shame: regenerating limbs and eyes, holding breath for a half-hour, running along vertical surfaces and upside down, subsisting on their own exoskeletons or the poop of fellow critters, and procreative propensities that are truly prolific.

While genuinely impressed with it as a

manifestation of Divine Engineering and Intellect, I am, nonetheless, still overwhelmed with an urge to kill a roach that I see right now: a peanut-sized, six-legged buffalo grazing on the great plains of my kitchen's linoleum floor. This urge seems innate, but it could be cultural, I suppose. And while it feels like I hate roaches when I attack them, I wonder if it really is hate that I'm feeling, because it only afflicts me when I am forced to share a confined space with them. Part of it may stem from a vestigial discomfort with being watched without my permission, an antique, pre-21st century concern. Perhaps I have a compulsion to rid my apartment of them because they are arguably my genetic superior or, even more likely, because I feel so much more important to them that their very presence in "my space," my Sacral spot of sun, my Accursed Share, is an affront to my pride in housekeeping. More grimly, I wonder whether my rage is rooted in a premonition of the horror to come – the overwhelming by bugs in the grave. Preferring to think of myself on the salutary side of ethics, I often rationalize my behavior by citing their propensity to transmit disease.

You can't rightly assess what's at stake unless you've been in places where the roaches have won. I've been in apartments in the South Bronx completely chock-a-block with whole clans of small, medium, and large roaches languidly conducting their affairs, comfortable in the notion that humans lacking advanced chemical weaponry couldn't eradicate their colony in the unlikely instance that they were to even try. Likewise, Taylor Mead tried to live peaceably with his "little friends" in a Lower East Side grotto whose every surface was outright gunked with roach poop. Taylor's "peace," such that it was, sprang from the Enlightened Indifference of a Dharma Bum, and it wasn't reciprocated—they bit him as he lay in bed.

Reminding myself that I am not at war with roaches, *per se*, I prepare to stomp. If just one of these creatures were to choose to live in harmony with a Universal Truth, could it be this one? And I think of Gregor Samsa, whose greatest mistake in life was waking up. I think of Gregor Samsa.

JIM GODOT
by Nick Regan

He used to be tall-boys and bumming cigarettes from anyone around. Ever since his parents smashed unto black eternity in the corpse Cadillac, it's bum vino and butts without filters. But he calls himself an artist. He tells everyone he was born and raised in New York, but the bloom of doubt from the suburban audience spurs when he promises he was practically raised at Max's Kansas City (he was born in 1996). He'll proselytize on inspirations, all specifically curated: black coffee, early Woody Allen films, the Stones' acoustic stuff, mid century furniture and low light aesthetics, hating Morrissey, cigs, the French New Wave. He's been talking for weeks now about a new album, but I don't think he owns a guitar. Recently, he's gotten into punk rock and even painted a canvas, "Rothko style," he says. Everytime he drinks, he mutters "Sotheby's or Bust: 2025." Every time he invites friends over for poker nights, the scumbags cheat him when he's manic rambling or living only behind his eyes. The scumbags swallow the large sums he always initially bets to impress, the money from the dead, the money for the bum vino fund. Sometimes he tells me he doesn't dream anymore. Sometimes he tells me he will sell this house in the suburbs and move to New York - Bushwick, or the Bronx, he says they have good coffee there. But I even heard from one of the scumbags that the nest egg in West Egg is crumbling. That he got ripped off trying to buy a Super 8 camera, or an Eames Lounge Chair. And now he's stuck with another heating bill in May, he doesn't know how to turn the heat off in the house. You can ask him how the funds are floating in the hand-me-down bank account but he always says money was rarely spent, and his material acquisition is an expression of rebellion.

Sometimes we drive by the house to see a simple orange glow emanate from one room. We think of visiting, but he broke the doorbell last week with a screwdriver. When you ask him if he's alright, he says he's "just okay" before handing you his copy of *Breathless*.

He'll never talk about his parents, or the last thing they spent money on: The Cadillac.

SAD SARAH: THREE POEMS

by Vokda Vida

1.
I'M AT THE DUMP AT THE DANCE ON
LAFAYETTE AND PRINCE ITS A WEIRD
SPACE FEELS LIKE A BAR FEELS GOOD IN
THE BACK THE DANCE FLOOR IS BEHIND
THE BATHROOM THE DRINKS ARE SUPER
EXPENSIVE AND THE CROWD IS BAD I
SEE THEM POINTING THEIR FINGERS AT
EVERYONE SAYING INCOHERENT THINGS
I SCREAM SHUT THE FUCK UP AND A
DUMB BEVERLY BASTARD FALLS TO THE
GROUND SHE STARTS MOVING TOWARDS
THE BATHROOM TO GO MASTURBATE

2.
I HATE MY TEACHER MR. YARNAL HE
SAYS MY ESSAYS ARE BAD SO I SIT IN
THE BACK HE SPITS WHILE HE TALKS
YOU CAN SEE HIS PENIS IN HIS PANTS
ITS NO COINCIDENCE HES THE SWIM
TEAM COACH A PERVE LIKE ME WHAT IF
PLEASURE IS THE SAME AS DRUGS AND
DRUGS ARE THE SAME AS ME?

3.
DARK DINGY BRAIN POWER PRIVY
PATHETIC SADIST SUCKER FUCK.

MOI NON PLUS

by Joseph Matick

Did you know the word negative didn't exist before school?

They teach that at university.

They are often saying all of this stuff, but nobody ever told me they were all beautiful. And nobody told me they were all of us. In us.

And I keep staring at this circle.

Which looks like us. It's like two wholes and this thing in the center...

I'll explain in person when I remember not to be present.

Which is impossible around you. And thank god for that.

And pie.

It's easy to believe in you.

I believe I'm coming home on May 7th.
Which is an example of a positive statement equaling a positive.
Two positives make a really good pie.

Man it's great to be alive.

That is an example of a sentence,
A life sentence to elect for

And remember when I went to a country and came back? Me neither. Like I never forgot home. And it happens in an instant.

I wish I were an itinerary but I am not.
Just a poem.
And getting away with living
is a hell of a way to die.
A way to die is an example of something nobody gets to live to tell you.

That sentence broke itself.

BOTTLED

by Jasmine Poulton

I tried to bottle
the scent of Paris for you;
an air specifc, evenly weighted with class and disgust
pipes and hot flour
mopeds and pastis
south, the cicadas make the air breathe like waves
when they fall silent I am afraid a tourist and abandoned
a storm or sun in breach
the cove today swam polluted, they say and I wish you wouldn't care
like I did not
when the hail hit our heads
the salted pool said stay
the thunder; safe until she cracks apart and if lightning finds us
here floating wet
as close to rain as the cicada to sky
it wouldn't be the worst way to go together.

BETAMAX
by Jeff Young

Inking her own skin, she summons sea witches
into her body, dazzle ships, eels, birds.
You can see inside her, the beautiful aquarium.
Inside her mouth there is desire, oceanic.
It comes pouring out in curses, salty, warm-tongued,
storm-weather, laughter like a night gull.
Of course, we're all in love with her,
she had us in her spell when she broke
into the lido, lay down naked in the pool, moon
bathing.
We watched her through the railings,
her erotic danger, the way she unraveled
Betamax cassettes, wore the tape like seaweed in her
hair.
She was our folktale, mermaid, mad angel of
pollution,
and when she grew old she still had that magic,
that wild danger in her tattooed body.
Now she sits at the supermarket checkout,
casting spells on young men – occult technology:
Maldon Sea Salt - *beep*, tinned tuna - *beep*,
Paracetamol -
swiping their man-souls into her wild lagoon.

GRAVEYARD EARTH

by Brent L Smith

I invoke all failed unknown dead
writers into me
I've got what all ghosts want
—a body

Make use of this flesh
Be a good little writer
You hear that, unheard dead?
I can leave where you left off
You dead loser
I am living loser
And I take your words

your language
your dead symbols
your archive
your thought-forms
I can wield them
I can make the dead walk
I let cadavers speak
I cannot speak

Through you my words flow
Through me your words flow
Let's make a pact in flesh & blood

Private eye in Hollywood Forever Babylon
Smith Smith vs. the Shadow Robots
Art techno deco
Stutterer's speech disrupts tech
"I'm—sorry—would—you—repeat—that—"

Pagan mod
Evil musician
Paralyzed from the neck down
Delivers performance with sound waves
And enslaves the audience to do his bidding

Old soul
I lay low
Off the digitized streets
I am purveyor of spirits
Hustler of the distilled essence
Supplier of intoxication
Instigator of inebriation
Enabler of immoderation
Middleman to slurred altered states

In underground bars
Subterranean haunts
Hollywood Blvd. bowels
Even our ghosts are stars

Saturn has returned
And I'm saving up money to open a tiki bar on Mars

I rip spirit from water
Stir in a glass
With sweet rocks
And you are become the possessed
To do the bidding of an old ghost

Older than history
Older than law

Older than Christ

Spirits just want what any ghosts want
—a body

I've lived lifetimes, kid

Orgasm spasm
Cum is death's ectoplasm
Isolation nation
Get outta this place
You married a monster from outer space
Death is the last dream
I've grown up into somethin' mean
Childhood summer camp over sacred intergalactic burial ground
Getting lost carries its own sound
When I was little I wanted to be a hearse driver
Now I make tips off mixing the Corpse Reviver

I've painted vistas
I've lived lifetimes, kid
I'm younger than you ever were
I'm older than you'll ever be
Last man standing

I've seen friends consumed
& devoured by the Blob
May forever live the hush-hush dealings of the mob
On this forever America
On this graveyard Earth
Reality is an inside job

INTRODUCING
by Craig Dyer

You could tell that in his youth he had been admired
A residue of that confidence clung to his proud bearing
It lay dormant in the wrinkles that now ran deep across his once handsome face
Like the scars of countless barroom brawls
He wore his weathered skin like a bragging right
As if his years labouring out in the elements
Were akin to the tribulations of a seaman
Who'd known nothing in life but stormy days and nights
He could weave an anecdote like he was casting a spell
His voice was deep, hollow, almost bass
A whiskey growl that could at a turn soften to a breathy calm
In which all tenderness was expressed
On a wave of stale cigarette smoke and the scent of ale
When he spoke meaningfully he did so articulately and lyrically
A trait he revered as that of his Irish birthright
His conversation was riddled
With references, quotes and the unabashed plagiarism
Of Joyce, Behan and Beckett
He clothed me in this literature
Before I was of age to fully appreciate it
Knowing that in challenging me
To the academic study of his well stocked bookshelf
He was providing an education that no school could compete with.

PORTRAIT FROM JUNE
by Ezra San Millan

I wonder if Joe Hughes means to drink a beer with me
around a fire on top of his lookout or if he is only words and a great faker.
Maybe a little of both. I like him more often than not.
His goofy black labrador Danny and his girlfriend Carol.
He is close friends with his ex-wife. His son killed himself.

Hold on, I just want to cross the street.
It's more of a conceptual idea than anything else,
the other side, crossing. There isn't necessarily newness even,
or should I say a symbolic crossing?

To look at the roses outside the church along the stones.
Or peonies or whatever they are. I don't know, flowers.
Begonias, petunias, a bush with little fluttery tuft balls in mild purple pink,
that man selling hotdogs and rice dishes from a cart.
It's supposed to be rather good.
It's sticky, wet, hot and overcast. So what's new with you?

Not too much. I stopped at the park a couple of days after stepping in chewing gum,
it keeps coming back to me. I sat in a dry patch on a wood bench and smelled my left hand.
A woman with cerebral palsy was carrying a little puff dog pomeranian in a sack around her waist.
It was bouncing around with exuberance and a look of fear in its eyes.
He licked my hand aggressively.

I wouldn't want to be that dog. She's had it for months and won't take it on walks
in public because it isn't vaccinated yet. He's a dog. A puppy.
But that's not why. I guess what I mean is I don't like the sack.

Anyway my hand didn't smell at all. But something in the park did.
I thought of the stringy gum from the other day and finished my coffee.
It was cartoon gum. Like cartoon pizza. I'm trying to take it easy.

My secret hangs in the air like invisible moisture.
I need to mail a rent check. That's about it.
Oh and I was listening to some Schubert later in the day.
I just love it when you're listening to a classical music recording
and you can hear the impassioned breathing of the musicians
in between the notes, string strokes and winds.

DREAMED REALITY
simulates the inner desires of the Drunk mind

by Miroslav Šujan

Time passed faster than capitalistic production, as I spent more days at home painting, taking photographs of strangers spotted on the streets, smoking cigarettes and thinking of myself and my dreams and art and life. I was stuck in a loop, in the space between so-called reality and imagination, between inner and outer worlds, between body and mind, between spirit and holy water. Daily events flowed like an independent romance-drama film that goes on for months without a break, like the book you don´t want to finish, like musical ecstasies on an LSD trip. And all those conscious realizations of universal situations escalated to me being in the dawn again.

There wasn´t a single spare seat in the bar. Timo didn´t have time to send back his human-being-passionate look, as busy as he was. But he noticed me and the subtle-soft confusion of my being. As he walked past me, he put a beer into my hand without looking and he continued. I didn't know how he did it, but he always knew what I was in the mood for. I sat down on the floor, in a corner, so no one would see me with my sketchbook. I put my beer on the ground, took a cigarette out of the pack, lit it and took a drag. With a leisurely sigh-exhale, I started to sketch like Jason Polan, capturing as many people as possible in as short a time as possible. To capture everyone´s unique existential essence through just a few quick-vivid strokes. To capture light and dreams of all beautiful people. Presence. After half an hour I captured exactly 143 people. And every single person left a piece of their persona, which cultivated me in a heavenly way. After finishing my third beer, an unknown guy came up to me, introducing himself as Nicolás. He offered his hand and I accepted with a handshake. He started the conversation with a compliment, that he thinks I'm an attractive young man, with a punkish-bohemian fashion taste, which he liked. He asked me if I wanted to join his group. He delighted me, and not just because he was French. But when a Frenchman tells you, you have *magnifique* fashion taste, it simply must be true. I pressed on to the others. I sat between two voice-pleasing long-curly-haired tall young men, Luca, and Marcelo. They were quite a large and loud pair, and I remembered them during fast sketching of their raw nuances, and with some I already symbolically fucked that night, because of our intense looking at each other during drinking, smoking, and drawing. We delved into many different topics and laughed constantly and my subtle-soft confusion from the previous days was rapidly released from me. It was definitely by the European-Mediterranean presence, the passionate-vagabonds and the confident masculine femininity. Feminine masculinity.

In the group of many beautiful and soul-attractive people that surrounded me, I sat down next to those who were my mirror. The deeply rooted, reincarnated image of myself. Soaking my soul and body in the smell and trance of cannabis, and looking at dozens of delicate, tiny flames, Timo put a record on the turntable. He couldn't have chosen better, because already, with all the sounds of the first song, my not-so-distantly-seen lost lust for life started to go beyond.

All the French immediately rejoiced and shouted to the whole bar *La Femme! La Femme! La Femme!* Psycho Tropical Berlin. The atmosphere of all the sounds and effects reflected the marvelous atmosphere of the bar. And with love and fun spreading around, another joint came to me. I took a slow drag and let it out. In the reflections of the eyes of everyone sitting together, I saw not only a life-infusing energy, but a blissful ecstasy of inner peace. I felt that I was living the lives of everyone who touched me, metaphorically and literally, and therefore I could understand everyone, they became part of me. The combination of French masculine feminine, Spanish-Portuguese hedonism, and Italian passion, was a source of energy to embrace and understand myself and my dreams within. We are one.

Everything was ethereally dissolving in me. I was with my parallel *I*. Tiny shiny dots flying over me, I walked into the direction of other states of metadreaming. And all in all, vivre sa vie. Il faut se prêter aux autres et se donner à soi-même.

THANK GOODNESS I GOT THE STUFF

by Parker Love Bowling

One million people are sick
One million people are sick
of sick people
Thank goodness I have been sick
for all my life
Thank goodness for goodness
Thank goodness for doing that
stuff on my face
and other stuff like that stuff
I like to do that too
I too am doing stuff like that *stuff*
but have only sick people
to do it to
Spend your money
now and then
Thank goodness I got the stuff
and plenty of sick to do

I AM PADDINGTON BEAR

by Matt Starr

i am a tiny
brown bear
named Paddington
and i like men

i'm not sure
if that comes across
in my movies or not
it probably doesn't
not my fault

believe me
i've tried very hard
to make my movies
more gay

i've had horrible
arguments with the writers
and producers about it

i've asked for outfit
changes to fall in love
with another male bear
to be just a tad more
sophisticated and they give me
nothing

somehow they've taken
a sex positive bear in real
life and usurped his sexuality
and turned him into

a sexless
asexual bear
which couldn't be
further from the truth
on the contrary
i have a very healthy sex life
i've got multiple partners
some casual
others more romantic
i love sex
and i'm not ashamed of it
and neither should my character be

SIX OF HEARTS
by Willie Crane

Instruction: *Have this read aloud to you by someone you don't know. Like your next door neighbor. Your best friend. Your lover.*

Close your eyes.
Take a deep breath.
Take another.
Take one more.

You are sitting on a bench. Next to the sea, only 50 feet from the water. Close enough to smell the salt, but a little too far to touch. That's ok. You're not wearing your swimsuit today and this is not a beach after all.

It's a chilly, sunny autumn day. The time is early evening or late afternoon. You make the call. Your view is one of a working seaside, with fewer ships than the large dock buildings to your left and to your right might suggest.

There's a small curvy path right in front of you that leads along the waterfront. You look up the path.

No one.

You look down the path.

Nothing.

You look in front of you, past the curvy path, and you see a patch of dirt and grass that runs right up to the retaining wall where the small waves lap up against it, saying something. But you're 50 feet away. And they're not sharing their secrets with you.

The bench you are sitting on is old. It's concrete. And weathered by the salt water. It has a large crack that is asymmetrical. You wish this jagged edge was a little more aesthetic. The bench has peeling white paint and missing a few chips and chunks.

You think about the people who sat here. What was it like when this bench was new? When everything was a long, long time ago? Does the view look the same now as it did before? Does the air smell as salty industrial as it did when there were more ships? Were the seagulls still poking around secretively as they are known to do?

The wind is still. We'll talk more about that later.

The sea is calm which is nice for this time of year. But there's something in the air.

It must be you. You are the only one here.

Who are you waiting for?

The seagulls who usually fly around here are somewhere else today. So are your friends. They could be far away in Portugal or just drinking down the road at that one bar that you could've gone to. But you are here. So here you are.

You know who you are waiting for. And you've been here for a bit. Not that you mind. You've got time. And you like the view. You come here often. Not everyday. But some days. And more often this time of year. Something about how the sun hits the water this time of the day. On a chilly, sunny day in the autumn.

Look in your jacket pocket.

You'll find three cards. You touch them. Without looking, you know they must be the right ones. They have to be. These are the only cards you got.

What are they? Mystical? Magical? Bicycle?

It doesn't really matter. You know the cards you have in your jacket pocket. You don't have to look. Take the cards from your jacket pocket. Hold them in your hands.

Do they feel different now that you can see them?

Lay them out. On the bench. The concrete bench with peeling white paint. The bench which is alongside a path which leads to nothingness and nowhere. The bench that looks out to the sea, where the waves lap against the retaining wall, whispering secrets that are out of range.

Take the first card. Hold it close and say just one word to it. You don't have to tell me what you whispered. That's between the two of you. And lay it right above the asymmetrical crack. This is your past. But don't turn it over. You already know the past.

Take the second card. Hold it close and say just a single word to it. You don't have to tell me what you said slyly to that card. That's between the two of you. And lay it right on top of this jagged edge. This is your present. But don't turn it over. You already feel the present, right?

Take the third card. Hold it close and say just a simple last word to it. You don't have to tell me what you said sweetly to that card. That's between the two of you. And lay it right below. This is your future. But don't turn it over. The future is not something to be fucked with.

Well, there you go. Aren't you glad the wind is still today? I told you we'd talk about this later. Look at the three cards. Past, present, and future. Without a worry of them being blown by chance out to sea or blown up the street to see your friends at the place where you didn't really want to go. And maybe that's why you are here. To turn over the cards. To see what you already know, but just need to know anyways.

SINCE I'M DEAD I GIVE GOOD HEAD

by Jack Skelley

Whip some skull on me, Bitch Boi: My bronze noggin gong, my uvula bell, my skin port to Gnostic Empress **Barbelo** Barbarella and her sacramental "redemption by sin." For within her heresies the scatological becomes eschatological.

They guillotined "I love you." But they could not cut-off passion. Prone in place, mouthing baby sounds, they lock ASMRs in coo-pillow kisses.
Now anointing the Neverland sips of her nether holes are the lisping lips of **Khloe Kylie Kenner** and **Kim**. They huff and they fluff, with her plumping glosses for pre-verbal labial sacraments of glug-glug, gargle & gulp.
(By the way, by "me" I mean she. By "they" I mean we. And by "I" I mean you.)
Holy fuck! I'm a **super-hawt** augmented Agnes **Moorehead** with ass implants! I'm weird Bewitched bish Endora whose bolt-ons rebound double cc's of bubble trouble.
And **I eyerollgasm** a cosmology of cosmetology.
In the upper Juliet balcony I bow, butt up, and command:
Lift this filly's flirty Tartan skirt.
Scoop & swat my Walt twat!
Careful, Romeo! You'll waterfall the floor with squish-squirt.
Hark! What yonder luscious lake windows holy heavens as we tally cums per encounter – maxing out one raunchy rally for a combined **13 !!!!!!!** Throat-pie counts triple for degree of difficulty: slosh wash, snug rub, tug-bath shiatsu in the upper esophageal sphincter.

Their epiglottis was Medusalicious.

Her carnal superpowers.

Her boulder-hard Gorgon gaze.
Her endoscopic plunger.
Her magical freezing of spunk-rock retraction.
They may snake-charm a totem-pole for eons, poised and posed to re-re-RE-release Mommy's Daddy juice.
But just one look, and Medusa Mama stoned him out of his brain. Post-orgasmic blackout bliss lobotomized *La petite mort unto liebestod* – a kind of craniotomy removing the tumor of consciousness.
As they stare at the mirror, they indulge dualities of objectification. Not just brain to body, but face to self.
And the self in all things.
Neurologically, biologically, is my face – the seat of my self – more spunkable than my physique? Might a skuzz-sloppy slut visage – eyes deadened in pleasure, tongue drivel dropping – reflexively out-hawtify even the shapeliest torso snagged in fishnet of green neon?

THE FOREVER NOW OF AHEGAO
(pron: ah-heh-gah-oh)
In dummy face a love supreme
Of cross-eyed stupefied submission
Into exaltation, a gaze into a glaze,
Mindfulness into mindlessness,
A terrible sublimity is born,
And our barbarous Queen Barbelo
Beheads the hydra algorithm of capital.

Ooh la la! A super succulent *coup d'etat.*

For the difference is between how a severed head perceives – a subject – and how it appears – an object: **drawn as a figure**.
Etched in the disappearing ink of cunt nectar, the eloquence of **Hélène Cixous**' *ecriture feminine* became the numb-faced mouth prowess of **Sasha Grey.**

Her male counterpart, Garrett Brooks, AKA **Girth Brooks**, engorged, engulfed his face & cranium – lips, cheeks, hair. The image of head alone liberates. It annihilates the constraint of object-model. It takes flight.
And levitating betwixt, transcendent and bi-gendered, **Kimber James** stages hermaphrodesiac transformations toward Bimbo dominions.
The only way he gets off anally is from full-on face.
She mouthed her taint in mother tongue.
She knotted her hair and woman-handled her.
They coaxed love blood repeatedly.
And in a dead head's anguish of desire, babbling the glossolalia that precedes language, spirit re-palpitated.

In The Greater Questions of Mary (third century CE) Saint Epiphanius – bishop of Salamis and a compendium of suppressed texts – recounts this ritual of **godhead**:
Mary took Jesus onto the mountain and prayed. He produced a woman from his side and the three began to gratify. And when Jesus, dumbstruck and cum-struck, fell to the ground, Mary raised her up and said, "We believe earthly things, that we may know heavenly things. The emission comes to partake of that from which it came."
Till the age of thermonuclear **warheads** exacerbated and extra-masturbated by melting ice-caps we de-cap the vein-popping of the mad male and let cooler **heads** of blowjob hotties prevail.
So now our Gnostic naughty-talk bans pronouns. Only pet names aloud. Cum when you are called....

1. Throat Boat
2. Twinkie Tot
3. Skankenstein
4. Wizard of Ooze
5. Cream-Filled Clitsicle
6. Her man Cumster
7. Cis Teen Chappie
8. Ass Fault Jungle

9. Kindergarten Coprophage
10. Miss Vaginatown

For the frenetic, mouse-like algorithms of marketeers may sputter, while love may teleport and pour the beloved thru shared pores.
For time transmutes. And less and less clearly do boundaries eyeball bodies enhanced beyond flesh, transcending Floor 13 to a trans-dimensional realm of moments sliced and sub-sliced in **Zeno's** temporal-to-tactile paradox of endless endlessness.
For at the end of days, the endlessness of endlessness is endless.
For language, which destroyed the prison of now, is, in turn, dumbstruck by skin.
For what is skin? Not a boundary, but a portal of 5 million pores.
For the epidermis, the largest organ of them all, wraps two into one.
For tears and kisses smeared Rorschach tests of blood and blackest black mascara.
And for, still more, even in TikTok Disneyfication, and a haunted Oz head, drone lovers will soar & hover, grateful in memories the fallen world would kill for.

I DON'T WANT
by Lily Lady

to live in a world
behind locked glass
in the bushwick walgreens
i boost the travel size lotions
b/c the big boys are locked away

the world is turning me wasteful
Lord, make me an instrument
is the first line of the St. Francis prayer

& just like St. Francis
i'm an iron deficient bisexual
grasping for God

it is in dying that we are born to eternal life

i like the sound of eternal life
b/c i'm not sure how long i can keep up
the age play

men like to say
watch this movie the character reminds me of you
like i haven't already seen monster

new client slaps me in the face during session
i guess being the board chairman of pinkberry
isn't so sweet after all

dov says stop thinking like a hooker
& start thinking like a businessman
like there's any difference

open the dictionary in my room
& behind the title page reveals a fireproof safe
life got better when i stopped learning new words
& started laundering new currency
i opened an LLC in delaware
called lily's luxury
b/c i want to live in luxury

i want to eat blackberries with jack skelley
to miss every turn on the ride to a trick
laughing w/ kat & singing hollaback girl

so if you see me in femme drag
it's b/c i'm about to get a bag
& if you see me dressed like adam sandler
the bag has been secured

in a return to love
marianne williamson writes
think of your career as your ministry
make your work an expression of love, in service to mankind

i want to be of service, an expression of love
but sometimes i get caught up

marianne goes on to write
every business is a front for a church,
to minister to the children of God

a front for a church, a front for a brothel
i never get caught up in semantics

i want to feel the innocence of the son of God

i want to feel the innocence of the son of God
i want to feel the innocence of the son of God

i'll start tomorrow.

DISPULQUE, ¿QUÉ VA A TOMAR?

by NC Hernandez

Marco Antonio Cruz, a photojournalist in Mexico City and president of the Procesofoto agency, died from a heart attack while riding his bicycle on Avenida Taxqueña a year into the pandemic. Before that, and just five days after the earthquake of 2017, a 40-year retrospective of his work was defiantly shown at the Centro de la Imagen amidst the wreckage outside, including photos taken during the aftermath of the 1985 earthquake.

La Hija de los Apaches, one of the oldest pulquerías in La Colonia Cuauhtémoc, opened in 1934 on La Piedad, later called avenida Cuauhtémoc. The bar survived several earthquakes, clinging to the islet that became La Romita, surrounded by a man-filled lakebed prone to rattle Doctores, Roma, Condesa, el Centro and Juarez. In 1987, Cruz and his Leica spent six months documenting the nocturnal goings-on of the place where Luis Buñuel's film crew once hung out on break from shooting *Los Olvidados* around the corner. The photos were exhibited in a show called *La hija de los apaches, la última pulquería en la colonia Roma, ciudad de México.*

Early pulquerías had names like Charros no Fifis, El Coloquio de los Megatorios, Los Hombres Sabios Sin Estudiar, Los Eructos de una Dama, and Aquí es Donde Sacaron la Muela al Gallo. The bathrooms, often just long urinals in a back corner of the room with a toilet to the side, were adorned with sayings like, "Todos pueden mear en el suelo, se un héroe, mea en el techo," "Por favor no arrojes las colillas de cigarro al inodoro (una vez mojados no es posible volver a encenderlos)," and the succinctly macho, "Puto el que lo lea." The facade of La Hija had two sets of swing doors between three columns of brick so it looked like a giant M. The simple barsign bore damage but still hung proudly, lit by the glow escaping the double entrance. Inside, largemetal pots filled with pulque sit inside larger pots filled with ice, and the mucousy substance is ladled out with cups that hang on the rim: some natural, some curado. It is clear from many of the photos that Cruz was prone to staying until the end of the party. And why wouldn't he? This is when the magical elements of pulque, not unlike the supposed dream state absinthe renders, begin to loosen the souls and bodies of its imbibers. Men pass out while sitting upright; in one photo a sleeping man with the fly of his blue jeans wide open sits under a collaged homage to Mexican boxers. In another photo a man is blocking his chin and winding up to slug the camera. Dancing begins and men try to outdo one another performing the splits. These men never see each other in the morning light—many never see themselves in it—but right now they're in the zone. The floors are filthy with spilled pulque, piss, and dirty shoe prints smeared across the tiles. A punk with a permed mullet and black leather biker jacket sits at a table next to the jukebox that can hold fifty 45's, probably blasting cumbias from a fuzzy speaker. At some point during Cruz's six month assignment, the jukebox must have been replaced, because in one photo it is covered in seventies-does-nouveau light up graphics, the top portion out of service, and in other another photo the machine is clearly from the 1950s. Either Cruz was there at the right time, or these machines broke down and were changed out often.

Certainly there has been documentation of pulquerias since the early days of photography, from the numerous early Casasola photos that show barely conscious campesinos leaning shoulder to shoulder, to the 1950s Nacho Lopez shots that blurred the lines between photojournalism and art, similar in tone to the photos of prostitutes taken by Cartier-Bresson or Sergio Larraín. The genre is not new, so what is different about Cruz's photos of La Hija? Perhaps not much in style—the photos are wonderful to look at—but what makes the collection unique is that La Hija may have been the last holdout among the plethora of former glory, surviving until the last round, owing surely to its pugilistic roots and proximity to the dangerous lore of Romita—José Emilio Pacheco, in *Las Batallas en el Desierto*, said it was the neighborhood of the worst robbers who would kidnap you, cut out your eyes, cut off your hands and tongue—its ability to resist modernity and trends, maintaining the same clientele of drunks, hustlers, queers, outlaws, retired boxers, and vagabonds, burned forever in celluloid by a man obsessed with his craft and the historical significance of his venture, perhaps also aware of his special place in those final days when the curtains of the analog world shuttered behind us.

Agua de las verdes matas,
Tú me tumbas,
Tú me matas.

JUST CALL IT WHAT IT WAS, THE 1970S

by Susan Bradley Smith

Lots of schoolgirls get lost in carparks after the night is over,
after the stars are done being everclear and start shining
in another hemisphere. They stand alone in these carparks
in the mothering rain, waiting for lifts that never arrive. It's
about to flood. The rain is really radium, it rinses them the kind
of clean that, for now, restores poise, fills their empty tanks
with courage, enough to get them home—it's a long, uphill,
country walk—and write sweet notes in their diaries that tell
truths which are also lies about the boy, the music, the kiss,
the pub doors that lured them in like a trapped wolf's smile.
The girl plucks at a wet daisy. *I know he loves me*, she thinks—
until tomorrow at school and the hopscotch of shame.
All the Same, she'll never forget him, even when her teeth fall out.

This is me, I am that girl.

Go ahead,

tell me what I did wrong.

MUTUAL ANGUISH

by Danielle Chelosky

to avoid catastrophizing
I dye my hair black
& I try (again) to write a novel—
my own Bell Jar to take advantage
of my current mental breakdown.
an illegible sentence on my notepad,
reminding me to read A Season In Hell
I sleep for twelve hours
but dream about work
it makes no sense: this deep depression
when I am your girl. what is there
to be so sad about?
instead of calling it masturbating,
we say we're yearning.
it's all good but then my vibrator breaks
& I'm in a hot sweat over nothing.
drunkenly, you take the long way home
to wave to me from the street
so I flash my tits in my stained glass window
but then I tell you to keep walking,
& I return to bed & remember my dream
of sleeping in a pile of leaves in the woods
& I'm like that guy in Sartre's Nausea,
constantly death-struck, puzzled at existence
I am a post-girl, I'm not fun anymore
I'm just an elongated anxiety episode
& Sartre doesn't really get it because he's dead
& you don't really get it but there's a chance that maybe
you do
because that's what love is to me: mutual anguish

I think about the time you were sixteen
puking in a high school bathroom stall
fourteen oxycontin & I am weirdly comforted
by your discomfort in living.
I make a list of things I want to escape:
my body my job my insecurities my future my relationships my sobriety my lease my fears my
ever-present anxiety my family my social media accounts my responsibilities my
irresponsibilities my inexplicable suffering my past
looking for a door
that doesn't exist.
so I undo your pants,
put you between my lips
like a cigarette, & at least
I know my purpose then.

LOVERS OF LOVERS OF LOVERS

by Fred Levesque

She twists you onto your front and kisses your spine
I watch cartoons in an unmade bed

Shame slivers through me for not being open
enough, spit down the middle, ribs pinned to the
doors

She whispers about the past you project everything
into the future- a black silhouette passing in front of
the moon

I can't sing over the noise in my throat and you can't
make a meal to save our lives

There's a plate of fruit for show there's a small fire we
can handle in the living room

There are traps set in the trees as you walk hand in
hand in the blue, oblivious.

But you bring her candy, you bring her ginger, you
bring her power cords and brittle feathers

What I am still doing here on this fucking couch in
the middle of the world? Take me from the shelf
My joints bend just as well– you reach across the
couch and grab her like she

Owes you the rest of her life. The projectile digs
deeper inward as the desire grows.

You paint a mural on our roof of formless beings in
love titled Marriage&Suicide and laughlaughlaugh

You twoheaded creature I bleed on your altar all
night to no avail– the radio plays songs that rhyme
with

Hallelujah. You cut your hair and trade it with hers.

You two are too beautiful for this patch of dirt.
If you could pass through me like vapor would you?

Well, will you? Oblivion, why don't you?

I'm stuck here until the shadow passes anyways you
may as well worm your way out of this mess.

I have no instructions for this new world, the maps
are blurred and soaked- she moans in your ear when
you lean in

She breaks up through text she invites you for tea she
fucks you in a car she disappears for halfascore

I reach for you in the predawn to find you staring at
the ceiling; dreams of wet organs float through

I'll need to squeeze something out of this like that
famous raincoat or that landslide song

I touch myself, I dream, these batwing spells shoot
out limp she's singing you folk songs in the dark

GHOST RADIO
by Jeff Young

We listen to mysterious transmissions
on shortwave radio, broken audio
of lost voices desperate to unburden painful secrets.
Once – for instance –
a man who prayed for a dog he'd killed, weeping.
Once a woman who watched her husband
choking but did nothing to help, counting final
breaths.

We listen to psalm-singers in the weather,
men trapped in sea ice,
seismic shifts in memory landscapes winter oceans.
Once – for instance
a grief-choir, the mournful hymns
of widows whose voices broke our frozen hearts.
An atmosphere of ghosts.

FORGET-ME-NOT
by Parker Love Bowling

Bury me in a field of
forget-me-nots.
that's my flower girl,
I do not wish to be
trapped in a casket.
If I have to be trapped,
let it be with you.

Don't kill me with
kindness.
Nothing phony will do.
When I am
dead and buried,
only think of me
when you're being
made love to.

Bury me in a field of
forget-me-nots,
and always remember
me by name.
Bury me in a field of
forget-me-nots,
and always love me
this way

VAMPIRE'S KISS, PART 2

by Shane McKenzie

Other boys would kiss her neck in hopes
of finding new points of pleasure
Only to discover two bite marks
pretend nothing is the matter

Skin so cold, making his blood warmer
Imagine she is a virgin
and you are

Our Father

Eternal hunger
She does not have
enough blood
to fall in love with

a mortal

It's hard to fall asleep
before the sun comes up
when there is someone else
in your coffin

Vampires don't write poetry
anymore

They just shoot heroin.

EYES ON THE CEILING

by Cynthia Ross

We faced another winter
Waking up wanting
Shaking and needing
Aching not feeling
Begging and pleading
Eyes on the ceiling
Legs that kept thrashing
And shallow deep breathing
Then there was stopping
The weakness of talking
And facing reflection, self judgement, rejection
Memories fading
Still you stood stalking
Resolve began waning
And heartbreak's cold calling
The harsh light of morning
Eyes on the ceiling
Aching not feeling
Hid in the cupboard
And waited a year
Re-entered with fear
Asserted control
With feelings and sadness
Time, it just passes
Eyes on the ceiling
Begging and pleading
Aching not feeling
Shaking and needing

JESUS LEFT AND LET US BE
by Dylan Lusetich

The story has abandoned the breakfast table
of rusted family years
and moved on
in secondhand embarrassment

We came on their altars
begged and bargained
at shrines made for one another

On a peninsula you and I
laughed at saints on the stained glass
fucked like angels,
gently and missionary

So that Jesus might leave us be.

In this famine we held each other
told funny sob stories
insults that went nowhere

We pissed ourselves crying
until the cancers set
no harvest to pray for
with no bounty left

As a boy I was told
this lack of noise was the voice of God
that silence speaking down –
one should be grateful

Sweetly I kissed your shaved cunt

and spoke quiet to the stubble
promises kept you'll never hear
to the You that loved Me

When I whispered 'God,
you made me believe in God again'
what I really meant was
Jesus left and let us be

THE ARTHOUSE

by Addison J. Fulton

The most recent exhibit at The Arthouse, John's art gallery, is a series that the artist painted in her own blood. It's a statement, the placard explains, on the inherent vulnerability of creating art. It's a bearing of the soul, of the self. Most of the paintings are bloody still-lifes of pomegranates and roses.

John stares at them, watching people mill about, gawking and examining and pondering. The exhibit brought in good money. The press was alarmed, wondering if modern art had gone too far. They wanted to go back to the good old days of the Mona Lisa, or at least the comfortable, bad old days of bananas stapled to the wall.

But the people were curious.

Is this the soul? Is it made of blood? Hamlet claimed art was a mirror. Was this the mirror? Is this his soul?

John used to want to make art, but found himself unhappy with everything he made. So, to stay close to art, he opened The Arthouse instead.

It's hard to see in a mirror so covered in blood.

No. This couldn't be it.

The Arthouse used to showcase normal art until John's mother died. It was a car crash, a bad one. Fiery. The mortician did the best they could for her corpse, but her will had called explicitly for an open casket. Even under the wig they gave her, John had to see the part where her skull was open and her brain had been removed. He was staring at the open void where all her memories and personality had been, but couldn't comprehend it. It was then he realized that the soul couldn't live in the brain where it could be so easily removed. It had to live elsewhere, like the Greeks and Victorians and other less-than-scientific, more-than-artistic societies had believed.

The Arthouse's next exhibit was called Arete/Catharsis. It featured a woman laughing for two hours straight, and then sobbing for two hours straight.

It was performance art.

It didn't help John find the soul.

The current exhibit, the one with the blood and the pomegranates wasn't helping either.

Dr. Doe had recently been sued for malpractice and lost his job. He was arrested for selling people surgeries they didn't really need. The surgery was expensive, but so is medical school. What goes around comes around.

Privately, Dr. Doe could admit that it wasn't just about money. There was a certain intimacy to surgery. Seeing the inside of someone like that.

Dr. Doe was a virgin in his 40s. Probably because he spent so much time doing surgery. He spent so much time doing surgery because he was a virgin.

A snake eats its own tail and comes to Dr. Doe looking for someone to remove a foreign object lodged in its throat. Later, it returns to Dr. Doe hoping to get a tail transplant.

"I need you to open me up," John says to Dr. Doe. "I need you to find my soul."

"What?"

"I need you to find my soul. It's for an exhibit. At

The Arthouse. Have you heard of it?"

"No. I find galleries pretentious."

"Okay. I still want you to do it, even if you think it's pretentious. To cut me open and find my soul. Will you?"

"I won't find it. I'll find just your intestines. And your liver. And the fat on your liver."

"How do you know there's fat on my liver?"

"You're an artist, aren't you? And a failed one at that. So you drink, don't you?"

"I do."

"Drinking makes your liver fatty. That's how I know. So I'll find your liver fat. But I won't find a soul. There won't be one, I'm telling you."

"For my life's savings, for all my assets. For The Arthouse. The building itself and all it contains, would you try to find my soul?"

And for no other reason than the fact he'd recently lost his job, Dr. Doe agrees.

The gallery is set up less like an art gallery and more like a slaughterhouse or an operating theater. Makeshift seating had been built on gentle slopes, like a black box theater. All of the frames were empty. As they look for the soul, John's organs will be placed in those frames. It's part of the art; it's part of the search. There's an operating bed with restraints, a metal bucket for excess viscera, and a metal dish full of tools. There's an audience. There's tension thick in the air. Baited breaths. What is art except for self-mutilating violence with an audience?

It's time to bear his soul. It's time to make art.

John is under the strongest painkillers that money can buy, but he insisted on being awake until the end. Hence the restraint. If he struggled too much, they'd never find the soul.

They start looking for the soul in the intestines. All they find is blood and partially digested food.

"I told you," said the doctor. "You're not going to find it."

"I have to."

They look for it in the heart next.

"No," says John. "Too much blood. Look somewhere else."

"If I cut open your brain, you'll die."

"It's not in the brain."

"I don't wanna look for the soul in your dick."

"It's not there."

"We're running out of places to look."

John wiggles his fingers in the cuffs.

"Sure," says Dr. Doe.

So they try the hands. Dr. Doe carefully runs the scalpel from the base of John's palm to the tip of his middle finger. He pulls the tendons out, one by one.

John tries to wiggle his fingers but finds he cannot. He can no longer make art; he is art. He can no longer make; he is.

"There it is," John whispers, reverent.

"This isn't the soul," Dr. Doe says, carrying one of the tendons to one of the empty frames. "These are the tendons in your hands. They just move your fingers."

"Yes, it is. There it is. Oh my God."

NIGHT AT L'ÉTINCELLE

by Joseph Matick

I'm over discourse and drinks and round tables and cyclical conversation
about music without making it,
about poetry without partaking,
Or dancing as if we don't.

I'm tired because it's late
and I'm tired of eyelids and gravity and gay friends and happy enemies
who don't know that two are mirrors
And no enemies
At all
And all round table Knights and nights
Without moons
Without eyes
They are nothing
And nothing
without you, I am tired
So many nights without you and with strangers
In danger of staying that way by staying that way
And effort without with or being
and being a fish big or small or not at all
and all the teachers and preachers who don't know we're in a school with a sister ready to crack a ruler on our knuckles and notions
And pretend poison and potions and love number nine and not number this
And I'm tired of this not being a number
The word this
It's a number

When will science catch on
And useless words
Which are all I can employ
and study and teach to budding young pupils
And they too have eyes
And they too need not brows or browsing
or screens or scholastics
But it seems like everything,
I am tired of
Words
These are all sentences without endings

HOT CORPSE
by Brent L Smith

On the South Side of Pittsburgh
Mad, masked Carson Street
Drinking at The Smiling Moose
Lonesome traveler
Bought a leather bomber jacket
Lighter than my others
Good for L.A. winters
Bought some charcoal to burn
Dragon's blood in my cauldron
I can't be a witch because of my dick
And "warlock" sounds fucking stupid
So call it what you wish
Time to clear the air
The Runaways and Iggy Pop on the jukebox
Cuz that's what the fuck I'm playing
Purifies like sage
Ooh wow. Ooh wow
They even have Ty Segall live
Deforming Lobes
"Love Fuzz" forever
Our music is fuzz. Thus our future is fuzz. All is fuzz
Or is it — Our future is fuzz. Thus our music is fuzz?
Whatever. All is fuzz
Relishing in solitude
Christ, I missed bars
The risk of Corona death is almost worth it
What else is there for romantic scum like me?
Well, I'll tell ya
Other than a book deal
And the occasional uninhibited doll,
Not much

How does that make you feel?
Simple
Words get me off, and getting off gets me off
You better be half the fucking writer you think you are
I am. I'm not
All our life stories end in rot
Drink enough liquor and your corpse is preserved
All drunks have vibrant corpses
That'll be the new beauty market to corner
"Did you see her corpse?" "Gorgeous"
"I want my corpse to look like her corpse."
A corpse hot enough for some sicko to fuck
Of course, I'm not that sicko
But such sickos exist
And if any corpse is going to be desired by a sicko,
I'd prefer it to be mine over my friends'
But I still won't get sicko laid
Though Death is all around me
Hanging invisible like the rock 'n' roll in this Iron City bar
It never touches me

EVERY ORGAN ERECT

by Jennifer Robin

The deadpan comedy of someone dying and their last social media post is something like, "I hate Elon Musk's balloon head," or "rutabagas give me runny poop," or even something ignominious like that one stripper passed out by a kiddie pool with twenties stuck in a sweaty g-string as a man who resembles a gnawed carrot is passed out by her side, five men who resemble gnawed carrots in a semicircle, Limp Bizkit T-shirts, wine coolers, freebase pipes and glassy smiles but someone was awake to take the pictures, some abstinent mislaid and possibly sinister biped, you can't stop scrolling through her photos to feel the age progression of the night before all goes black, or is it white, this page is intentionally left blank, this icon-flesh abandoned to the path of sudden pregnancy or fist-sized tumor. Final social media words: "I'm at the station need a ride NOW." "Amsterdam makes me sneeze." "ngl I find Adam Driver sexy." "6mg risperdol with watermelon don't want to be found" reminded of the one who dies with an unfinished meal or unflushed toilet; the currant bun cooled and the urine outlived him; a fine line to fondle between paucity and glamour; spyglass dissolution means we need to see the bones emerge from the pocked promise of youthful fat; our myths can only arise in finite zones; homunculus crucibles, small and alchemically incomplete bodies treading water, nostrils and mute eyes as captured between overdose and squalor; and we swear we care to our creations as we stand above the rim, gaze with every organ erect

IT'S DEAD BUT DOESN'T KNOW IT YET: I have a plant that has been slowly and horribly dying, from a lack of light that my apartment currently can't give, and water that I did give, abundantly, a monsoon of misplaced affection until its roots turned Fellini-ochre; a rich mahogany rot. In a panic, I unearthed it and trimmed off the dead parts. I baked its soil in the oven until the air smelled like an amalgam of armpit, oyster, peat. As we do with dizziness, tooth pain, and listless pets, so I did with this plant; I looked up its nature and needs, all too late, and discovered what I had done wrong. In one plant discussion group featuring a man named Only Peanuts whom the others found overly aggressive, a poster said something about my genus, a plant from the arid zones of South Africa that should have never received a monsoon: "It's dead but doesn't know it yet." Even as its roots rot, the uppermost branches with their pulpy green petioles spiral towards Earth's bounty of photons, a seemingly endless berth of sun. I checked: It takes eight minutes for light to travel from Sun to Earth, two months for root rot to reach the uppermost branches, whose leaves, when they first emerge, appear to cry in slow motion like the beaks of baby birds.

Self-Contained: Is Earth

I imagine you a skull, I imagine you many things; full moon masturbation and what we choose, the small lives, the ones we recognize are beyond salvation, but no one wants to hear that. Colors soon to be demolished, lives unpaired. The Syracuse rap marathon where I masturbated fifty times in two hours, because I was in a house alone with my mother and the lyrics to every song on the radio were about the way skin hangs over curves of muscle and fat like gift wrap and the breathing is what every drumbeat urges. How can anyone not see the loneliness? How can anyone be so self-contained? Is Earth.

Grave Capacity

Remember those vinyl blow-up dolls, sometimes in the shape of Goofy or Mickey Mouse? Remember the smell when you got your lips up close to the blow-hole? The leaking of air, the repulsion and compulsion all at once; almost a hunger to cover the leak, force in breath, make the animal fill to capacity with lung-warmth? And then the sealing! The quick sealing of the umbilical spout, to be sure the air will not escape. Our toys must remain firm, but we love them when they are deflated. We, those afflicted, even as children, with a grave capacity to feel the inanimate have needs.

RAMONA, WHO KEEPS THE PAST AWAKE

by Fred Levesque

Ramona the laughter booming in the dark
while we run up the to pasture where the white
horses are sleeping
slips into the chamber when I'm least expecting it
What keeps the past awake is the picture of the
memory
As much as the memory of the picture
Ramona the future comes cascading down the stairs
like so many buckets of fake movie blood
And your hands are bright red but of course it
couldn't be you
you would never
all lace and teacups

Ramona of course the sky is full of stars and dripping
Across your back like a loose knapsack
I'm pixelated and zeroed in- look at what you've
done
As convincing as a river coming out of the deep
black

Ramona of course the median grow wild flowers
And we have to be grateful when the sun turns
them into brittle sculptures
The crooked love note origami you burned
Didn't mean to start the field fire in the middle of
our lives

Ramona of course of course not you
You're a collapsing star,
You're so open that everything's inside out again

Ramona of course I understand
You're an adult and you're in pain
And that should be enough

Hand blocking the sun, reaching and reaching
Just beyond
 out of sight and mind
As if we could get rid of it like a nickel in a pond

STELLA

by Vokda Vida

I'll be twenty-nine at the end of the month, which means I was born in 1980, which means I only know how to drive automatic. It's pouring. I smell the grease on my fingers and start chasing my memories of useless junk. I was born in Jersey City to a Polish father who washed windows for money. I liked making clothes, baking cakes and reading magazines. I piled them up high on the rug in the living room. I spent my childhood cooped up on the top floor of a high rise condominium with a single mother shattering vases and rolling around in dirt shards of glass that would leave cuts on my legs and arms I liked how it felt. I'd bang the glass on the windows hoping the glass would crack. I don't care about talking I walk past the tire shops and bodegas the streets are filled with older men they follow me I move faster and faster the wind is blowing the street signs rattle the doors to the warehouse are wide open. I turn right and enter. The store is sparse a lot of room to breathe half of the lights are burnt out. The left side is full of cheap neon costumes, stripper heels, leather gear the ride side another room with magenta and blue tile filled with dildos and butt plugs. I'm looking through the costumes the stripper thongs i want so bad I grab a beige one size XS. The register on the platform is covered by a plexiglass barrier with an opening at the bottom where you place your cash or card. I put down $15 dollars. a man screams WATCH WHERE YOU ARE GOING BITCH I'm blind you asshole a lie i tell everyone a lie so they feel bad for me and help me i put on my smoke black double thick sunglasses that cover my eyebrows a face full of freckles no one can see pain is an emotion that i release i have fun rubbing my tongue up and down my cheek pleasure is the same as pain and pain is the same as a mirror that can contribute to self-hatred and self-love so i smash it hoping the glass will break hoping the glass will shatter i'm blind i can not see and my mother would say what you dont know can't hurt you the day before i died I was fighting about having fun i couldn't solve my problems anymore i grabbed a gun from my big black leather bag inside a mess lingerie tags empty Poland Spring bottles the floor was covered in water from ice that was melting from the storm earlier i put the gun away convince myself don't do this not yet too soon i walk into a mini mart get a pack of cigarettes boss hasn't seen me in forever they will give me the pack for free boss you're one of my friends please give me a pack for free i sucked his dick in the basement after hours i get the cigarettes for free i get a grilled cheese for free my mouth wide open tears rolling down my face i start clenching the cigarette like a man with no teeth. I grab a pigeon with my fist and throw it in a flower bed on the sidewalk under the track on Jackson ave across the street from the adult entertainment shop they sell lingerie bongs and poppers I go there because the lights wake me up I go there because I'm bored I fried all my brain cells in the heat keeps getting hotter and hotter I'm sweating on the couch with a $20 box fan on full power blinds shut tv on watching porn back to back to back bdsm latex fetish slave excitment now extinct the walls in the room can talk they scream yell and taunt i'm scared that I like it I wake up the next day covered in sweat wrapped in my sheets with the voice inside my head you better come back go to the bathroom put my fingers down my throat and vomit all day long i faint time doesn't exist anymore lust is grass i burst into flames I dance and overhear the news from last night about the man who fell in the water and swam to the shore covered in bloodwater and now there's bloodwater in my backyard.

WHERE WE USED TO SLEEP

by Kurt Eisenlohr

Long ago and far away, the youngest of my brothers had a friend named Monroe who would stay at our house for days/weeks/months, and on one occasion Monroe came in hot with a 90 minute cassette he'd made consisting solely of the acid era Beatles ditty I Am The Walrus, a 4 minute and 33 second recording laboriously transferred, spin by spin, from vinyl to four hundred and forty-four feet of magnetic tape wound on a wheel going round in circles, and right before falling asleep each night on a couch in the basement he would press PLAY on a boombox that had auto reverse

A Side/B Side/A Side

I AM HE AS YOU ARE ME AND WE ARE ALL TOGETHER

the song repeating itself again and again at a volume subliminally audible throughout the shared heart of the house, an experiment Monroe was conducting to determine what effects relentless absorption of the lysergic composition might have upon his fledgling songwriting chops (I'm guessing) while inadvertently altering the DNA of the dreams of all who dwelt there (again, guessing).

The duration of the experiment escapes me, when it began or when it ended, or if it ever truly ended at all, but it was an honorable undertaking, and I am grateful that the forever-loop we experienced at the hands of Monroe was Lennon's I Am The Walrus and not say, Ob-La-Di, Ob-La-Da, which could only have led to madness (my own). No disrespect to Paul McCartney, or the song, or the idea of life going on (and on and on and on) because I so wish it did.

THE AUTOPSY
by Craig Dyer

I am a garden of colourful anxieties
In which the absurd flaunts itself

Irrational
Incongruous

It bares its scars
and lifts its skirt

It spits between its fingers
and masturbates

It screams my name
and whispers fears

It's time for a purge
a clearing out

Clothing off
up on the slab

The autopsy

Now I'll open up

YESTERDAY OR YESTERDAY'S IDENTICAL TWIN

by Alain Schumann

Anger is the colour of this miserable Tuesday I haven't left the apartment for
2 consecutive days
the filth is moving around me, gathering for secret meetings and plotting
behind my back
after all there's only one of me
against so much of them
the sink is breeding civilisations
their numbers are growing
the king is grumbling on the royal single bed, annoyed that he has to chew his food before he can swallow it
I can't even remember what I ate 5 minutes ago unless I burp
nothing is of any particular interest to me boredom breeds a lot of hate
I get angry at my bladder for reminding me of basic human needs
there is no end to my self loathing I want a dream tank to go sob in
but there are no tears
only rage
followed by total absence of thought navigating the apartment in impeccable choreography
The automation has made a redundancy of the engineer
his mouth and ass are still needed though the story of a tired mind gone on vacation I'm all anger and no brain, foul and untamed but not prejudiced
I distribute anger rather arbitrarily everything deserves

a piece of it and there's plenty to go round
every other hour I find myself engaged in combat against inanimate objects
idle shoes get yelled at
toothbrushes get bent out of shape
books get tested for sturdiness -
I kicked Henry Miller out the window in an almost perfectly shaped arc
only to shuffle down the stairs a minute later cursing to get him back
give me back all the things I drove away with anger

I'm a presbyopic moon
scintillating over the earth
I'm a stale porcelain chamber pot full of shit that hasn't been changed in a while
I'm a dog on an invisible leash guided by the fragrance of backsides
I'm an indoor bunny with rabies
and I've turned against the golden cage I'm a black hole, turning all to nothing
I'm a pregnant Nessie about to give birth to something hideous
incubation has made me insatiable
give me something in a skirt to feast on

I don't know if every day is truly worth living
the days seem wasted on me, and I on them I am aware
that the world can't afford the broken
and so I long to be
fixed.

THE END OF THE AFFAIR

by Sophia June

It is not only the end of the bar, but also the end of summer. It is August and we are drunk on dusty bottles of champagne, humidity, and heat lightning.

Ari is standing behind the bar pouring herself a draft beer into a pint glass covered in greasy fingerprints. Her leather corset is coming undone, the pleats in her skirt have loosened, but she still looks like she could get cast on the spot for *Coyote Ugly*. Only she is not a bartender. She is a server, and the only reason she is allowed to stand behind the bar is because in a few hours, it will be closed forever.

The glass overflows with foam, beer dripping down its sides like the tide coming in. I remove it carefully from her hand. She tries to grab it back from me and in doing so, backs into a wall of glasses, shattering two coupes.

Ari looks around to see if Paul, the shaggy-haired bartender and his nice flight attendant girlfriend, whom she despises, are nearby. She stage-whispers: "Did anyone see? Am I too fucked up?"

"That's a question only you can answer," I say. I am so tired of people asking me that.

"Actually, it's a question only you can answer," she says. She has a point.

"I love you," I say, because I don't know what else to say, and kiss her on the cheek.

I tell her the narrative arc of the night has concluded and it doesn't matter who she kisses or who puts their hand on her back or thinks her hair smells good. It doesn't matter if Paul leans in and whispers in her ear that he's going to leave his girlfriend. We're past the point of the night where good things happen, and I'm trying to get better at identifying when things tilt over that thin line.

She stumbles into the wall and I tell her I'm calling us a car, but she wants to stay. "It's the last night," she says. "Ever."

"We will be going to bars at the end of their lives for the rest of our lives," I tell her. "If there's one thing we can count on it's that bars will close."

Steve, the owner whose indie rock band had a one-hit wonder in 2012, and Jeremy, the owner with small hands and an abandoned fiction career, gaze at a wall of Polaroids of staff who've worked at the bar over the last five years: a good run for most things outside of a human life. Steve puts his hand around the back of Jeremy's weathered neck and kisses him on the cheek. They toast to each other, whiskey running down their chins.

People are squeezing each other's shoulders, and nestling into nooks of necks, and wiping tears and popping champagne corks. All of this because a delivery guy slipped in a puddle of spilled canola oil and broke his leg, spiking the cost of insurance. Everything was going to end anyway, but nobody thought it would end like this.

"This is where everything HAPPENED," Ari says, gesturing to the cracked aqua vinyl booths, the neon Miller Lite sign, the walls covered in faded postcards. I don't know how to tell her that she will think this about so many more places. Some of them will have stickier floors than others.

Since I don't work here, there is a gauze scrim between our understanding of what this night means and I don't feel like lifting it. I remember when the first bar I loved closed; I remember feeling like it was where everything happened: the phone numbers scrawled on the bathroom stalls, the kisses by the ice machine, the maraschino cherries that stained my fingers like blood.

I don't know how to tell her that there will always be a manager whose band had a one-hit wonder and there will always be a bartender who doesn't like his nice girlfriend, who will pull you into his lap and whisper in your ear, telling you that you're the one he's been waiting for his whole life. There will always be delivery men who will slip on stairs and cockroaches in the well. There will be many broken glasses.

Instead, I raise my champagne to her, which we're now drinking in pint glasses because nobody wants to do the dishes. Steve comes up the stairs, the same stairs that were the downfall of the bar, with another case of wine. Everyone erupts in cheers.

"Finish it all," he yells.

I drink the last sip in my glass, kiss Ari on the cheek, and walk out the door. I have been here since noon and it's now dusk. The sun is slinking towards the sidewalk, and it's impossible to drink it all.

ADJACENCY
by Karen Schoemer

You stand over me,
trying to understand me.

I'm sorry.
Stones are proud.

Canal water stagnates
but old engineering methods

hold. Shadows
on the towpath are hungry.

Crow calls
pass like boats.

If I say, "Now the bullfrog
trills forcefully," I'm insincere.

Air is between us,
shifting our perspectives.

The tender ruined things you see
are overwhelmed by proximity.

If I say, "Now the phoebe's
squeegee interrupts me,"

I am not [blank]
[the word for being]

but adjacent.
I am trying to be human.

JOHN WATERS AT THE SIGMA SIGMA HOUSE

by Nick Regan

"I would qualify this all as camp, especially the mounted deer head decorated with Coors Lite... But I can't even smoke in here?" John radiates in a familiar tone, so akin to cursive letters among daily, staunch and capitalized banter of the Sigma Sigma house.

The Pope of Trash, adorned with his trademark Little Richard mustache, had relinquished his position at the local Baltimore penitentiary to help guide a new audience cursed by society's ills. Although the former death row inmates he taught to act out their violent fantasies through writing were a product of a system gone mad, the high-fiving, 'Who do you know here' party bros were a new breed perverted by a source unknown to John: Daddy's Money. They would be a tough crowd to educate - as misogyny, aggression issues and a collective penchant for verbal harassment were backed by a culture steeped and validated by their mythological legacy and the occasional pat-on-the-back 'Attaboy' approval by Father when they returned home to the villa in backwards caps and vineyard vines.

Yet, John's vocation had not been dismayed by the unruly rich kids. Over the first few weeks of his presence at the Sigma Sigma house, he had cemented his status as the friendly weirdo, and even helped one of the boys buy a tab of LSD from the campus punks without being ripped off. The boy was so grateful, he even said John could be a plus one at their lawn party in late May. John knew that the rest of the bunch hunted competition. He mixed one of their annual events, a case-race to finish a thirty rack of beer, with a viewing of his work, *Pink Flamingos*. Some of the new recruits got sick during various points of the film, but John was there to hold their backwards caps as they expelled the dining hall food into the buckets provided by the ringleaders.

Questions about John's sexuality provided a great deal of tension between the boys and the legendary filmmaker. He dedicated a lecture, turned to Q & A, to educate the ignorant and answer the questions any member of Sigma Sigma had about his sexuality.

"Gentleman, my door is always open," he told them as the allotted time for the lecture closed in. A few recycled jokes passed like a game of telephone as the immature and uneducated sat before the Sultan of Sleaze. But some grew empathetic and reveled in their newfound wisdom, excited to mansplain this new knowledge to the women in their finance classes.

"Thanks, Mr. Waters," many said, as they ushered out to an afternoon of skipping classes and playing Madden.

As the fall semester concluded and the Baltimore air grew colder, John began the process of packing up his things and contemplating his experience, wondering if he made any true impact on the lives of these boys. The day before the last of the finals were submitted, John clasped his suitcase and headed down the trash-laden stairs of the Sigma Sigma house and towards the door. In the main room, where he spoke to so many J. Crew catalogs come to life, a large crowd of fraternity acolytes stood together. John paused in his departure when they all met eyes.

One of the boys began, and soon the others followed in chanting, "O Captain, my captain!" A single tear rolled down the cheek of the Pope of

Trash's face. They all soon concluded, some wished him well with a handshake, others with a hug. John was then handed a thirty rack of Coors Lite on his way out as a token of their gratitude.

"I love all you Balti-morons," John remarked with a smile.

"We'll see you at the May lawn party, Mr. Waters!" a few replied back as John exited the Sigma Sigma house.

I WAS A CHILD

by Jasmine Poulton

My pleases were not good enough plain
they needed
to be pretty: iced
topped with imaginary cherries
I was a child learning
I should beg
for what I need
and must manipulate my words to earn myself worthy.

MY CRUCIFIXION SCENE
by Dylan Lusetich

Jews don't believe in love
It's why they're smarter than us

I'll drag myself across a desert
and play the role I was meant to

An idiot who throws himself against the holy land
and screams,

'I'm gonna act out this crucifixion scene
and I'll film it,

And they'll believe I did
One thousand takes over for someone I don't even love'

And I'll look up at you
and you'll just sort of laugh

WINGED WARRIORS

by Cynthia Ross

When part of you dies
With people and time
Something survives
Darkness and light

Morning denies comfort
Time marches on
Like foreign soldiers
Singing sad songs not sad enough
In perfect time

The streets have changed
Melodies burn my brain
All minor keys and discord
Sung by angels who are not angels
But winged warriors
Carrying messages

Winds that cannot breathe
Memories etched in pain
Sad songs without refrain
Whispered stories without endings
In ancient language without words

There is no safety or salvation or sunlight

Hummers hum
Love dies again
Over and over
Repeating lines
When part of you dies
With people and time

BILLBOARDS BEHIND BURIAL GROUNDS

by Shane McKenzie

She had a thing for
dead guys

She will be
the death
of me

Don't put my ashes
in a box

Bury me
in a
cemetery

by a tree

Where a pretty girl
can sit in the shade

and touch her
legs

and cry about a man
she can't

marry

BROKEN GHOST

by Jeff Young

So much damage in his face
you could see the wiring,
the entire machinery.
You could even see his afterlife,
the premonition, the broken ghost.
More tree root than child,
more butcher's dog,
the only one who knew
where the bodies were buried
and who was doing the burying.
One memory though, strange in its beauty –
I watched his hands, those brutal fists
holding a bunch of marigolds:
such tenderness, such gentle pleasure
and then he turned to look at me -
eyes shining, pollen on his eyelids.

IT'S COOL WHEN A TRAIN IS SIMPLY A TRAIN AND NOT A HUGE ROLLING CAN OF COORS LIGHT

by Kurt Eisenlohr

No such luck today
but I did hear a man
shout the following into his phone
and it sounded like a poem
so I will present it as such:

Couch full of hate
Coffee table full of anger
Dirty dishes full of lust

You can keep all that!

ACID VEGAS
by Brent L. Smith

They don't even have gambling
In the Cosmopolitan
...very cosmopolitan
We start feeeeeling good
Our senses redline
The world becomes italicized
The noise becomes amplified
Knocking 'em back
Our drinks sweat
Hoping the booze would dumb us back
Down to earth
But it's no use
Through crowd
Past the hectic flow of Marquee
& the refurbished cigarette machines
Dispensing single-serving art
Along the walls and down an empty hallway
A silence hits us like a BANG
Temporal nexus —
Walking by giant red stilettos
& towering aboriginal figures
Some with horns
Bearing spears and armor of gold
They guard the pantheon
Of ancient Vegas
Vampira
Howard Hughes
Frank Sinatra
Mia Farrow
Ann-Margaret Smith
& the forgotten queens of 60s burlesque

Once desired and world-famous
In some dazzling mausoleum now
And just as quickly as it came on the vision faded
As all heavenly visions do
Back behind us in the time fog
We submerge down into the lobby noise
Among the jaded waitresses
Barkeeps
Cigarette girls
& go-go dancers
Like a glimpse of Summer 1969
Manson Family visions
Of Hollywood poison invading holy desert
You ever hear him speak? That Man Son...
"I live on the ground
I live on the earth
I don't live where you live
I lived in Hollywood and I had-all-that
The Rolls-Royce and the Ferrari and the pad-in-Beverly-Hills
I had the surf-board and the Beach-Boys and the Neil-Diamonds
And the Rob-Snobs and the Bee-Skees
And the Elvis-Pressleys-the-Best-of-Bestleys and all them guys...
The Deena-Martins and the Nancy-Sinatras
And 'will-ya-do-it-to-me-Honey? I-hear-ya-do-it-good'
And that kind of 'will-ya-come-up-to-my-House-later?'
So, I went through all that
And I seen that was a bigger
Prison than the one I got out of..."
We hit the strip

where tourists wander around lost
taking pictures of everything
and peacock showgirls stand around
charging for poses and you look up
and Britney Spears is forever entombed
in Planet Hollywood
The landscape of Vegas reflects
its schizophrenic inhabitants
Spawned one day out of the dirt below
The skyline has raised and so have the stakes
Cost of living
Whatever
There's a new glass ceiling
and all the wealth is on the penthouse floor
Implode the old and erect the pre-fab new
While "Feel So Close To You Right Now" plays on every corner of the
Strip
Like a bad radio dial
A dressed-up distress beacon drawing in coveted youth
In this dead frontier
— future invading the present —
Only the young bring anything in
And they aren't young for long
Like a 3D holographic centipede god
We curl up to and writhe around
In a beautiful sequin cesspool
With Liberace on the piano
And lost in the blue sea
Of our Liquid Crystal Displays
We're all just trying to do something simple —
Connect...
The great big desert mirage

Is big enough to fool us all
And the only real crime
Is to act like you're above it
But the Vegas commercials
Tell you one thing
And reveal another
Nothing stays here
There's nothing here for anything to stay
It stays with you
And it stays with you no matter how high your tab is

CREATIVE DIRECTORY/TAXONOMY (EXCERPTS)

– New York (East Village/West Village/Bushwick), July 1989 and April 2023
by Richard Cabut

1. Unstable street is steadied by an utterance.
2. Poetic line advances. Impossible connections.
3. One image follows another – interfacing fluid mirror.
4. Uncapped bottle of beer – smudged lipstick.
5. Uncapped lipstick – smudged bottle of beer.
6. Sex. Holy prayer cards on bedside cabinet. Holy cards close to chest.
7. Poetics governed by impulse. Yo Vito!
8. Dialogue: I'm not scared! You're scared! I'm not scared.
9. Taxi ride at night. Link with words en route. [Timeless immobility].
10. Dialogue: You were going to tell me something before all this happened, what was it?
11. What does anyone want? To offer a raw-boned shoulder twisted against the world.
12. Phone booth. Man cries. Love is dead. Vibration travels from star to star.
13. Voodoo shops in Lower East Side. X marks the spot. Line between intuition, refusal, affirmation.
14. Extended dream sequence of bondage vignettes. Some words spoken: But I don't FEEL anything.
15. Everything is learnt from the night – weight and density of thoughts.
16. Your skin is so wonderful. Image of self. She said. Image of nylon.
17. New star visible via angel's eye.
18. Vertigo of modern sensibility. What lies beneath; the neural pit and electric crackle.

19. People believe in dread more than they believe in allure. They howl.
20. What do you want? Control of own mystery.
21. Life in the city is a balancing act: Hysterical crude illusionism. Dazed abstract psychology. Theory of misfortune.
22. Well, if you put it like THAT!
23. Question: Is the Parisian void better than the New York void?
24. Title moves between two different senses. Promise of explanation of some particular movement.
25. Image always bleeds faster than cash.
26. The glamor business: D and F ride through town. T asks M about the book she is starting. Magazine pages being turned over. Text against text.
27. This is not just an object, it's just an object. Archetype against archetype.
28. Violence of slow motion sentences. [Disappearance].
29. People live in a documentary style. Action is always quoted.
30. People have been working all day. Point of view: reverse shot only.
31. Dialogue: I will remember this moment for the rest of my life.
32. The street: Disney plus bodily fluids and open wounds.
33. What do you want? Control of your own misery.
34. Alone in a room. Turn light on and off. On and off. You can see the story.
35. Someone quotes: 'Frigid people really make it.'
36. Desire in eyes like dying words. Full face or in profile.

37. The street is: Cinematic paradox. Are you certain?
38. The history of the future. Hegel. (Hey girl). Nostalgia for the lost.
39. Dialogue: Wow! (of course)
40. The meeting of a client's need. Life with subtitles on.
41. Question: Do you know how to pony?
42. Classical chiffon evening gowns. Woman's mouth open, eyes half closed. Uncertainty of interpretation.
43. Heat. Blurry and unfocused. Associations of the taste of old, used pornography.
44. Architecture is masked figure.
45. 'Purism' tattooed on thigh. Fiction is an under developed pretext.
46. Atmosphere: old 50s film. Movement between fragments/frames is called desire.
47. A new star visible. Its Creator did not disdain.
48. People quote Dante all the time: Predestined turning point of God's intention.
49. Wildest fantasies forever unfulfilled but always exceeded. Something else.
50. Movement towards something constantly absent. Travellers' tales.
51. People say Modernist film theory is the key to everything.
52. Freudian dream symbolism. Buildings dissolve as soon as approached.
53. Fixed aesthetic of street corner – inviting departures rather than arrivals.
54. Fact of flesh without flash. Pre-visual freedom.
55. Genuine religious feelings. Gears of consequence.

56. Disquieting lady makes escalating demands. Asks about philosophy of the bathroom.
57. Club Kids are full of prevailing climate of parochial formalism.
58. Dialogue: When I first met you I thought I might be dying. I thought it might be good.
59. Older man dreams of breaking into warehouses on Hudson River piers.
60. People simply love the anti-humanism of structuralism.
61. Steam engine unconscious. Loneliness. Neutral neglect.
62. Do you want art about art and signs upon signs?
63. Dialogue: They're collapsing, too… in perfect unison
64. Artists' lofts for rent. Artist imitates the viewer. Vacuum in an airless room
65. Everywhere. Walk on part – TV staging.
66. Dialogue: I can't look at you and breathe at the same time. (Extreme solitude).
67. People wonder if it's OK to have 'a sympathy for the abyss'.
68. Violence, how fluently it comes. How simply it cures you. Absence and the fast heartbeat.
69. People like eroticism through lack of context. Reflection and blankness find common identity.
70. Golden hour natural light and low sun sinking down on empty warehouses. Escape from worn out iconography.
71. Dialogue: Stop! Mama!
West Village. Woman in shop doorway reads battered copy of Tuli Kupferberg's 1001 Ways to Live Without Working.
73. Club Kids in platform boots tell dealers to fuck

off. Snort face powder and blusher.
74. Sleeping in freshly wet bed. Moving beyond the embrace.
75. Arc of thin legs and bare arms. Distance from the feeling to the face.
76. Dialogue: Each and every attribute of society is my annihilation. (Folk joke).
77. Question. Images like jewels (momentum). Do you still believe in that?
78. Dialogue: Well say something.

OP CIT

by Karen Schoemer

The wind is made of glass. Its sound
its smooth glass sound divides the lake.
A row of houses on the opposite shore

is unreachable as Henry James's Paris.
Children's voices call as if they're playing
in those unreachable uninhabitable houses.

The wind is made of glass. It divides the lake.
Thinking is on one side. A row of houses
mysterious as if they're playing on the opposite
shore.

I push the glass barrier an inch, half an
inch.

Why push it? Why not let it stay? Why not
rest alongside the mysterious glass gateway
between the lake and a similar idea

in someone's head. The wind is made of glass.
I make mistakes and in those mistakes are
jewels
and in those jewels are sinister unreachable
houses.

Why not push it? An inch, half an inch.

ALSO OUT ON FAR WEST

Milton Keynes UK
Ingram Content Group UK Ltd.
UKHW010857010424
440421UK00004B/365

9 798988 735441